your touch on my skin • luca l. huntzberger

AF199098

your touch on my skin

- luca l. huntzberger

First paperback edition: January 2020
Printed in Germany 2020

Published by BoD
Books on Demand, Norderstedt
ISBN: 978-3-7504-0944-6

for my aching heart

contents

luca l. huntzberger

TO LOVE

it was like a roller coaster ride:
i was shy at the beginning

next, you took me in your arms
and gently caressed my cheek
and my forehead

told me how beautiful i was
screamed and laughed with me
when all of a sudden,
you left me alone

because it was all over again

i'm drinking the exact same cocktail he
and million others do
i'm breathing the exact same salty sea air he
and thousand others do
i'm watching the exact same sunset he
and hundreds of others do

but he's the only one making me really jumpy
with his blue eyes
with his bright smile
with his beautiful hair
no one but he can make my days
the most beautiful in the world

your touch on my skin

you are the one i really can count on
the one i can escape to if i'm in trouble
the one who dries my tears
and puts a smile on my lips
the one representing the closest electron
at the nucleus of an atom

this is you. i love you.

we both lie on our backs – naked.
this strong feeling occurs
when two people who are loving each other
from deep down
stare at the same night sky
observe the same shooting stars
listening to the sounds the crickets make

with this feeling inside of me,
i turn to him.
it wasn't that bad
everyone said to me.
it wasn't hurtful or anything
because he was nice to me.
he was gentle, careful
and wonderful.
he is wonderful –
that's why it was pleasurable.

i put my head on his chest
and soon begin to sleep.

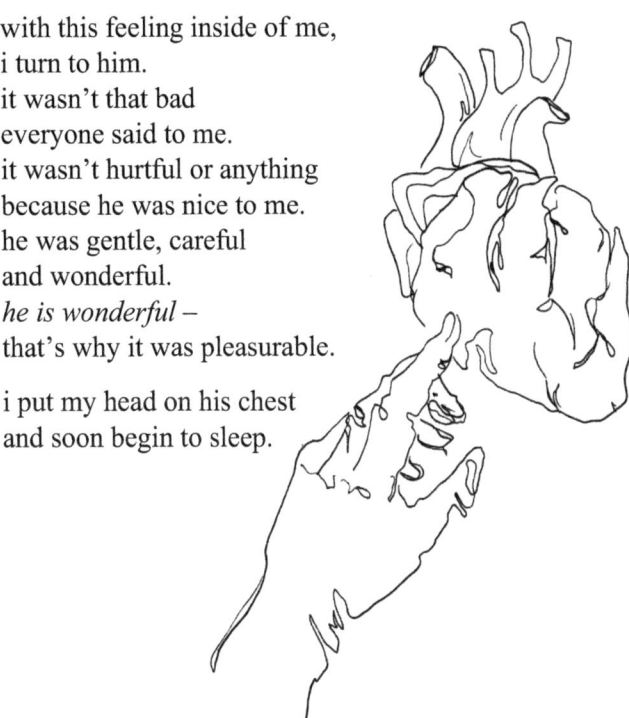

'remember that: during the day,
i watch over you as the sun.
even if you can't see me.
remember, one day – if the clouds
take your view and everything seems grey –
i will be there.

remember that: i keep watching over you at night.
i am one of the millions of stars
in the night sky and will shine, only for you'

she said, kissed me and closed her eyes.

your touch on my skin

the *greatest happiness*
seemed unapproachable
to me to this day
not even nearly tangible
what words cannot describe

but now i know what it means:
to have you in my life

one morning you will get up because of the chirping of the birds. peace.

the sun is shining through the windows and you think you can start right away without any interruptions. stupid thought.

you turn enthusiastically to the side and stare at your phone screen just to check if everything's alright.

oh. it's this someone you admire. that one person you never want to lose. someone you strongly love. but actually, you don't even know who this someone actually is.

but that doesn't matter because this someone has texted you the sweetest message of all time. you can no longer lift your gaze from the single letters which together can only mean one thing. i love you. heart emoji.

you look at the picture, someone sent you yesterday, again and again. why does it always have to be people that cannot be here? people who physically cannot sit next to you right now. people who always cannot kiss you right now.

but just because you can't see and feel someone in real life right now doesn't have to mean that this couldn't be your future someday.

the bird, which always remains unreachable for you, makes you come back to the present. but it's only a bird with wings.

you were like the few words and the melody
you know from this old song
you haven't heard in a long time
and soon begin to google for
you were like the joy after
having searched for it days and days
and finally seeing that song cover
it's everywhere the same
sometimes you lose sight
sometimes it needs time
to find to each other again
but in the end, it's like
retrieving a forgotten one –
making the bound even stronger.
i love you.

'which three things would you take to an abandoned
island?'
all of a sudden, i see someone in front of my inner eye.
'only him.'

i really thought it was hard
exhausting and competitive
but when you realize
that there is something between you
that you don't feel with anyone else,
you are meant for each other

it doesn't matter how many
potential people are still out there
the right person is sitting right in front of you
take your chance
and suddenly
it felt really easy

we're both sitting on the balcony.
with a picture-perfect view of the eiffel tower.
with a wine glass in our hands.
at midnight.
we look at each other closely and for a moment
everything is weightless.
everything is beautiful.
because of you.

your touch on my skin

sometimes i wonder
that i'm actually
very loud
for an introvert
i look around,
see you,
and know why

sometimes i think i'm stuck in a dream
everything so beautiful, colorful and calm
yet so unbelievable
'because i've never been
that happy in my life before'
i say to you
while i feel the grass below me
the warm summer wind
blowing through my hair
having the taste of my favorite liquor
i drank with you in my mouth
and *everything seems pretty alright*
finally

when i see you, time has passed
time we spent with other people
time i wasn't with you
when i see you, you have news
news that you've told other people
news that have nothing to do with me
but when i see you,
i know this doesn't matter anymore
all i know is that i'm with you
that this is the strongest bond
i've ever had with a human being
know that he will never break
because you are my *best friend*

going to poetry slams with friends
driving around town with good music
going out and meeting new people
travelling, drinking, dancing.
this is called life.
unconditional life.

your touch on my skin

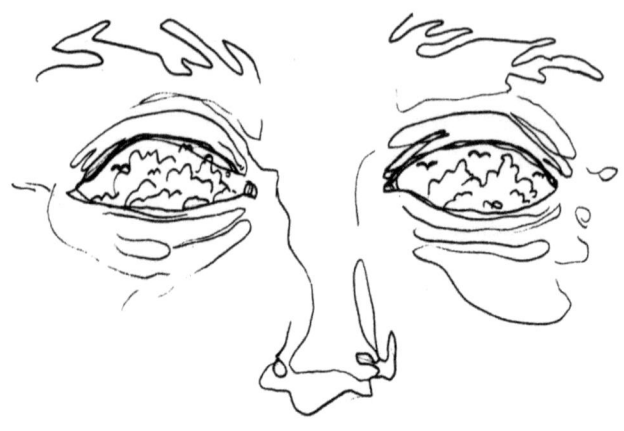

i'm opening my eyes
in front of me: endless road
behind me: the same

i turn my head to the side
and see him driving the car
see his almost perfect, flawless jawline.
his blue eyes, his full lips,
his bushy eyebrows
his hairy, muscular upper arms.

i gently kiss him on the cheek, he smiles
and for a moment
everything feels so god-damn
weightless

'you've inspired me.
you inspired me to get up every single day
to work on my big dreams
to be who i really want to be
thank you. i love you'

i say to my grandpa, close his eyes and
kiss him good night.

i never realized
how beautiful flowers were
until you made me go to the park with you.
i stood there for ten minutes
and couldn't believe that i had failed
to recognize how beautiful
they could be all those years.

why do you write
poetically dissipated letters to everyone
but yourself?
why do you take the time
to put your deepest feelings,
love, appreciation and hope,
out to this someone
but won't take a second
to do the same to yourself?

why should your life
depend on another person –
why should you
center your life around that person –

instead, put yourself on the highest step and
appreciate yourself for one moment
start to write that love letter to yourself
with the most *honest and appreciated words*
you can express
because: why not.

your touch on my skin

i don't wanna be that someone from school

instead, i wanna be that someone
who kisses your soft lips
who you share your
most mysterious secrets with

indeed, i don't wanna be
just a stranger to you anymore

take a breath
and shortly think about
the following question:
'what are you grateful for today?'

your touch on my skin

sometimes i think i'm a prime number
because no one wants to divide myself
except me
and then i remember there's another number
the only number left
number 'one'
and that's who you are

before i met you
i disgusted cold water
such as that icy pond in the winter landscape
where we went on holiday every year

you showed me that cold water
can also mean a refreshment
on hot summer days
when i lay next to you in the dry grass

i'm standing on the platform with you
cool summer air envelops our bodies
the yellow-red sunset kisses us good night
you hold my hand and pull your
smoky cigarette with the other
i give you a kiss
and another one
and another one
and i know i'm gonna have to let you go now
even though all i want is
to have you with me tonight

i wouldn't dare to say
'i dreamed of you'
to you
because you're the one
who is pretty
yet so shy
who is close
and yet so far away.
you have no idea
how much i love the idea
of me and you
talking, laughing,
holding hands, kissing
no, you will never know
because you're that one
who is everything
yet so unknown to me
and that's why i'll keep dreaming of you
to have you by my side

your touch on my skin

luca l. huntzberger

TO HURT

alcohol is not a nice drug
makes you feel like shit a day after
destroys your body
shatters your brain in little pieces
we all know that
but sometimes – only sometimes

it helps me
helps me to forget
the fucked-up world
we live in

you accelerate
without waiting for me
you decide to go right
when i want to go left
you decide to turn around
and left me standing alone

'and i think you're the *most bitter person*
i've known' he texted me once.
sometimes, this sentence
repeats itself in my head
and i still keep grinning about that
since *you knew nothing about me*

giving someone a sign
whether to believe in something
or rather letting it go
would be really helpful
in some situations

your touch on my skin

the veils that cover the moon
are the veils that extinguish
the light in the night.
i can't see myself.
can't find you because
these are the veils
that deny me any access to you.

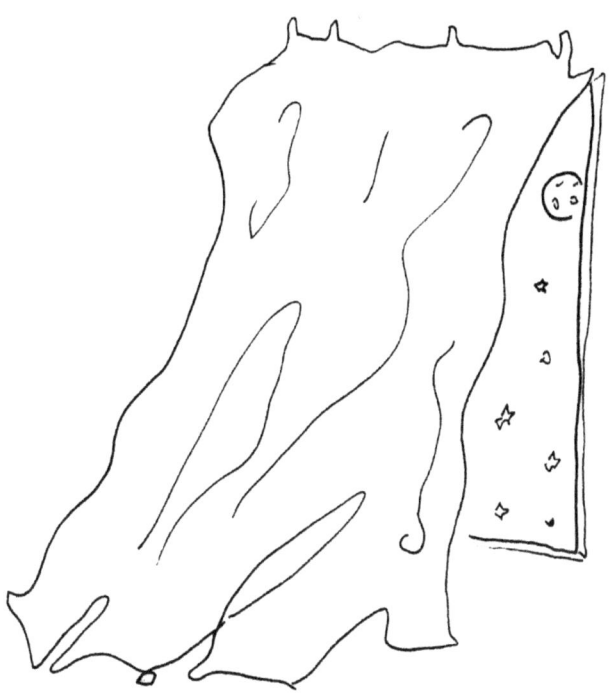

breaking up with someone means
deleting screenshots
deleting sweet pictures
telling your friends:
telling *the story* countless times
crying
sleeping
crying
sleeping
cr–

'i love you', he says
i look him in the eyes
but my heart hides the words
that won't come out

society has to learn that
even what you don't see still exists
– 'no need to be like that.'
that it can destroy you
– 'no need to be like that.'
your friends, your family, your loved ones.
– 'no need to be like that.'
even though you cannot physically see it,
doesn't mean you're a liar
doesn't mean you're faking.
– 'no need to be like that.'
is my pain also invisible to you?

i see your back's scratched
i see your bruises over your legs
i see the pain in your eyes

i ask where this is coming from
you say it is nothing
i look at you deeply
all i want you to know now is
that i'm here for you, okay?

your touch on my skin

fuck – fuck – fuck – fuck – fuck
i hate you – i hate you – i hate you
leave me alone – leave me alone
goodby–

i saw him
he came to me
he left
i cried ashamed

your touch on my skin

during the day, i keep smiling
i keep laughing
i keep ignoring
as if i didn't care

but at night, the facade falls apart
because i lose the strength
to hide the emotions i tried to burry
and weep me to sleep instead
to be able to play the same game the next day again

your touch on my skin

i still remember it very well
when we've decided to do more again
in our free time
to find to each other and
close that gap again
yet we let this gape open
even further
drifting apart cannot be stopped
if it isn't supposed to be like that

not being able to tell your crush
what you really feel for *him* / *her*
because you fear the rejection
tells a lot about yourself

your touch on my skin

you look so happy
every time i see you
i observe your hickey
and abort the attempt
to get to know you

it kinda feels like *sorrow*
when i think about the feelings
i had for you
when i was deeply in love with you
but it sometimes also kinda feels like
disgust i have for you

i lie next to you in your bed
i smell your perfume
i once loved you so much
i look into your blue eyes
i once fell in love with you
i kiss your soft lips
i had my first kiss with you

but realize there's nothing left for you
that there was something that died now
that i don't belong here anymore

you confused me
to that extent that,
all of the sudden,
you texted me
so friendly, so lovely
yet so odd for me
you confused me
to that extent
that all i could think about
was you

you, when i awaited your
hasty glance at me during lessons and
you, when i awaited
 your messages during the day,
you, when i wanted to fall asleep
and thought about
your beautiful voice

when i finally realized,
all you have successfully done
was to turn my life
upside down

your touch on my skin

sometimes i wonder how much money
i must earn to escape
escape work
escape family
escape friends
escape lovers
escape you
to be free
let go
bye

i once saved you as 'my love. *heart emoji.*'
today there is only a telephone number left

your touch on my skin

once in a while
i have a look at myself in the mirror
sometimes with a good feeling
sometimes not

in these moments
i eagerly try to smile
but it kinda feels like
you've overridden not only my muscles
but also my soul

he's talking about cars
and i'm talking about arriving.
he talks about cars
and i talk about travelling.
he talks about cars
and i talk about studying.
he's talking about cars
and i'm talking about *leaving*.

your touch on my skin

he still keeps texting
when all i want him to stop
when all i want to go on
he still keeps texting

you're asking me if we're ditching school together
– and you know i'm saying yes because it's you
you ask me if i can do your maths homework
– and you know i'm saying yes because it's you
you want sex
– and you know i'm saying yes because it's you
i'm asking you if you can come over
i'm saying everything sucks and
only you can make it kinda bearable
but you're busy. you're *sorry*.

your touch on my skin

she is not beautiful enough they say
she is not caring enough they say
she is not feminine enough they say
so she decides to tear out all her hair
making her not feminine enough
hair by hair
blood runs
tears flow
tears flow
blood runs
hair by hair

your touch on my skin

i dreamed about you and
that was the first time in a long time
that i had you so close to me again
and when i opened my eyes
reality reminded me that
you're never coming back

you sit in front of your work of art
a fragile girl holding lilies in her hand
when you only have the urge to rip it up

but when i look at it,
i see what seems to be
inconspicuous for you
because i see her mysterious, sad look
but also the beauty in it

when you only see yourself

your touch on my skin

the honest truth is that
we've never been together
we've barely dated
but to this day, i can't forgive you
for having had something going on
with another guy

luca l. huntzberger

what has been missing between the two of us
that people need to be happy
to love each other –
what was really missing?
and was it my fault?
was it yours –

luca l. huntzberger

my phone is jammed under my ear,
quietly, i lie on the bed and listen
to your breathing
i notice you've fallen asleep
and say what i've always wanted to say to you:

'i love you, baby. really. but i don't think i can do this.'
the words sound sharp and at the same time sad
on the other side of the globe
and with tears in my eyes,
i hang up.

your touch on my skin

you are not even two meters
in front of me
but the distance between us
is immeasurable
and never bridgeable

you yell at me and soon
i no longer hear your words
i only feel your anger
which hangs like a cloud between us
all i want is that it disappears
want all screws of our relationship
to find their way back into their holes
but soon i start to realize
that there is nothing left than rain and
screws coming loose

your touch on my skin

when i'm around you,
i don't feel like i belong to you
it's that feeling when there's
a battle in my stomach
and a lump in my throat
it's that feeling when i want
to hide in my mother's protective arms
and long to be a child again because
everything seems playfully light there

one day, you just begin to ignore me
you just start developing
hatred for me in you
say: *'you are not good for me'*
and call me *embittered*
while i'm trying to fix everything
trying to connect to you again as close friends
when you suddenly
cut the bond that was between us

'i hope i'll see you still regularly', you said
when all we had in common was over.
i knew that we won't because
hope isn't the right approach to that

i take pictures of everything
when i sat next to you on the bank
and filmed the restlessly moving waves passionately
cause the moment wanted it that way
and you were there

i turned to you and captured your smile
and yet i have become aware
that you can't catch anything
that you don't have someone forever to yourself
no matter how much you want it to stay

i so often sit there
pressing my hands against my ears
brutally, desperately, sadly, furiously, painfully –
because you're too loud
you're too negative
you're too differently minded
you're like a stranger
to me
you, you are north and i am south
you, you are the cold and i am the heat
you, you are the grief and i am the joy
you, you are the pessimist and i am the idealist
and all i can do is trying to make you quieter
in my ears, on my skin, in my head –
and hope to be free from your unbearable noise
someday

isn't it
sip
the last
sip
opportunity
sip
to forget
sip
sometimes?
sip

moral injustice ...

these are two words so abstract
yet so true when you've been in
that one situation
two people actually so lovable
take sides against you together
insulting you
yelling at you
denying your dignity –

is it only my fault or just
moral injustice?

you know – you are the reason i can't sleep tonight
it's because the things you said
it's because the way
you expressed those letters
forming syllables
forming words
forming sentences
forming insults
it's because the way you looked
and the indifference
you showed afterwards
i don't know if you have
a black and stony heart
i don't
i don't know
if you are stuck or traumatized
i'm not
so please
respect that for once in a lifetime

your touch on my skin

sometimes i would prefer to live under a bridge
the cold, grey stones
would radiate more warmth
and colors than you do
and the sealed place
which would give me
more freedom i have
ever felt with you
sometimes i would
love to break out
and sometimes is now just
only a *matter of time*

luca l. huntzberger

TO REALIZE

your touch on my skin

i have a distanced relationship to my mum
when it's about love
maybe i'm prudish
maybe i just want to talk about it
but she once told me that
sometimes, it's better to just
clarify things
to say what needs to be said
and to let go.
saying goodbye.
and this is one of the wisest things
i've heard in a while

i recognize that place. charlie, my doggo.
'do it or we will', he says.
bizarrely, i can't open my mouth.
maybe i physical can't –
maybe i don't *want* to.
fireworks in rainbow colors
illuminate the evening sky
'gay – gay – gay – gay – gay'
is what the writing on the horizon says
everyone is around.
my family. my friends. the whole city.
i cry and sob and cry and sob and cry and s-
after i realize it was only a dream.

your touch on my skin

it is really worth it
to make yourself more beautiful
with photoshop to get
more likes with it
when you find
sadness and dissatisfaction
deep in your heart?

luca l. huntzberger

we would all
– proud as we are –
call ourselves
highly intelligent human beings
yet we are on the bottle
every night and
cry ourselves
to sleep

your touch on my skin

i so often realize habits
that i have adopted from other people
with whom i no longer exchange words.
that hurts even more.

they lost everything
they lost their homes
lost their jobs
their identity
to see them smiling and laughing happily
after all this happened shows me
what life really means
what strength really means
what courage really means

you press the new button and there you are: a whole new white page. no words, nothing.

you decide to start a new life determinedly. without all your *enemies* and all your fake friends. without all those people who don't really like you. now!

you think of that word again which is called: *selection*. you agree on the fact that it sounds honestly terrifying.

so, you start at the bottom again without having spoken any words, without having made any new friends.

to begin a so-called new life seems simply unbearable at the beginning. but within the next second you begin to appreciate what you already have in life. your family. your few friends. yes, maybe you only have one or two good friends. but these ones matter! these are your second family. people who are backing you, who deeply love you.

so, you know: everything will turn out well. and you ask yourself: what was i afraid of? the fear of being alone? the fear of being in a spiral of loneliness and unkindness? or was i afraid of the future?

these things seem unimportant and irrelevant now
because everything's alright. more than alright.
everything's perfect. you are surrounded by lovely
people. you are focused only on things that make you
happy. you let people who have bothered you behind.
thinking about that makes you smile.

*so i pull my laptop closer to me and i move my fingers
determinedly and confidently to the keyboard and type
the following: i'm standing on the mountain and look at
the landscape peacefully and tacitly. the birds are
chirping and the flowers are growing rapidly.
everything seems just so vivid, bright and just colorful.
just like me.*

tears are running down your cheeks
and – cold as they are –
are falling on your hands
and your scarred arms

it's all dark – not only outside –
but you're breathing.
you are still here.
you are doing okay.
that's a reason to move on.

a long time, i thought you were an angel
maybe *my* angel
infallible, wise and innocent
almost godlike in behavior
when you let Satan carry you down
and made a pact with him

your touch on my skin

i noticed how silence kills me
i noticed that i want to skip unpleasant situations
just to come to the beautiful ones
but that's not how live works
you can't run away from the negative things
and *you kinda showed me that*

overthinking means
creating uncountable scenarios
one worse than the other

it's like a cube that divides itself into further cubes
which divide themselves into further cubes and
at the end, there are innumerable before you and
you begin to lose your mind
when you only need to think about the initial cube

your touch on my skin

running away from a crucial question
can end up being painful
like running away from a wasp
and still getting stung in the end

luca l. huntzberger

every time i get to know someone new
i start to search in them what i loved about you
want to see *your character* in them
want to find *your intellect* in them
want to find *your beauty* in them
but I'll end up only disappointed myself

your touch on my skin

sometimes i rack my brain
about the question
if i can't find my
love of my life
because of my *type*
but then i will remember:
if i like you, i like you
there shouldn't be any *type*
brown hair, blue eyes, muscular
but just the warm feeling inside
your chest and the voice telling you:
yes, baby. he's it.

i think it's really evil
that universe has given us the chance
to be dependent on someone
one out of 7.53 billion people
almost forever

but never forget that universe
has also given us the *chance*
to forget, to let go, to love again –
to find another one out of billions of people
it won't be as easy as the first
but makes it much more hopeful

maybe i can't believe it today
maybe i laugh about it today
i know that there is going to be
a hand to hold
someone who puts me ahead of everything else
someone who is going to be there for me
until the world dies
someday

not being able to put something
into words when it comes to
expressing feelings is okay
not being able to understand
one's feelings
because it
doesn't make sense is okay
it all takes time
it's human

your touch on my skin

i look into your grown-up eyes
that don't look into mine
wait for your head to turn
into my line of sight
wait for you to look at me
as fervently as i look at you
and finally, you look at me

my feelings play crazy,
i start imagining what it's like
to have a relationship with you.
what it's like to kiss you.
but in the next second
i am aware that i will probably
never see you again.
that your gaze was probably
nothing more than
just a gaze.

why has waiting become such a big part of our lives?
we wait until the bus
picks us up in the morning
we wait until the ringing of the bell
releases us from our day
wait until the pizza is ready
wait until the clock says
we should go to sleep
sleep and wait until the alarm clock
wakes us up again
wait until it's finally friday
and then wait until it's monday again.

why can't we wait less and live more?
why can't we just let the
door to freedom finally be open?

your touch on my skin

sometimes the screams and shouts
from my parents
are ringing in my ears
maybe this is exactly the reason
why i don't want to raise children
because i fear to be the same –

does it taste like blood?
does it taste like unconditional love
or like the shattering pain afterwards?
is red my favorite color
only because of you?

your touch on my skin

it would be seriously
a whole new experience
to have a free trial to new things
when you are socially anxious

luca l. huntzberger

i don't think the spell
'you cannot divide by zero'
only applies to numbers

what scares us today already?
death? it gives our lives a meaning, a goal.
school? it will pass sometime.
galaxy? not important enough.
what really scares me are
feelings

she's addicted to alcohol
he to cigarettes
she has a food addiction
he a sex addiction
no matter who and what
remember: never judge
but try to help
at the right time
and you contribute
a lot to the people
secretly asking
for the exit
out of the
misery

your touch on my skin

TO ACCEPT

stop thinking about him
stop stalking him
stop following him, finally.
i try, i really do.
i wish i didn't care.
but i do.
because that's me.
i care.

do you also find yourself
sitting in front of your phone
looking at old pictures
with your friends?
sitting in front of it
and keep smiling weirdly
and remembering the situations
you took them in?
remembering the fun times
when everything felt simple?

but do you, at the same time,
also find yourself sitting there
having tears on your cheeks
when you realize that,
what you see, is long ago and
just history –

your touch on my skin

i'll be sitting on my bed
listening to the sound of the dark night
and be asking myself
why i keep loving you
why i keep needing you
why i keep thinking about you
after what you have done to me
after what my friends told me
after what I tried to convince myself of
and be answering that
it's one of my sinful urges

we used to share our most secret secrets
we used to talk in school
we used to greet each other in school
we used to wish each other happy birthday once a year
we used to ignore us
we used to hate us

every time i listen to this one song
i get reminded of him
his smell and his beautiful smile
because he loved it
because it was our song
and now –
it's just *another song*
i painfully have to ignore

do you know how hurtful it was
to realize that grandpa wasn't picked up
by some angels to heaven
but just died painfully
in mother's arms –

your touch on my skin

uncountable times i checked if
you already read my message by now
until today: no reply
just a 'seen'
and a block

sometimes i really hate myself
just because
i cannot believe
how much i'm addicted to people –
people that are in a whole different league
people i barely know
people that seem to be attractive and
people i've never seen before
sometimes i really hate myself
just because i'll be crying over
the disappointment that comes
with every hurtful message
in the end
because of my trait
of loving too fast

i know i'm stuck
every day the same,
everyone the same
but at the end of the day
we long for the *regularity*
because we aren't able
to control the spontaneity –

so, we're so comfortable,
we're moving on
with the shit
we'd love to
throw overboard.

i think it's okay to cry
i think it's okay to mourn
mourn the good old times

i think it's helpful to be heart-broken sometimes
i think it's helpful to experience
experience failures and mistakes

i know that it's good that we have such times
i know that it's good that we can learn
learn from mistakes everyone makes

i'm sure that better times will come soon
i'm sure we can see it
see the rainbow after the stormy rain

perceive the happy after mourning
perceive the good after the bad
perceive stability after struggeling

your touch on my skin

he so often said
'i love you so much'
but he never has.
he never tried.
but hid behind those words.

sometimes, you wish
everything would be fixed
you put all your strength
into fixing it
keep struggling,
keep bending,
keep yielding
but at one certain point,
you need to let go
need to understand
that it's not meant to be
let it go.

does a person find your sore spot
a nerve that shakes you and lets you lose control,
then don't shy away from it
don't shy away from tackling the sore spot,
even though it has hurt you once
we all have to go through this certain pain
to be able
to love ourselves in the end

sometimes,
and you can't do anything about it,
lust leads oneself to
precarious
dangerous
painful
unsafe
stupid
situations you've never wanted
to be in

you cry for help
you scream for an ending
but lust decided to never allow
an ending and
any help
for you

at some point, i'm gonna break the boarders
at some point, i don't want to
be pressured to drink alcohol anymore
at some point, i don't want to
be pressured to talk to you anymore
at some point, i don't want to
be pressured to be around you
to listen to the same music
to live here
to breath the same air as you anymore

at some point, i'm gonna break the walls
hindering me to live my life
the way *i* want to

luca l. huntzberger

sometimes i don't know
what road to take
which conclusion to draw
and what to change –
but that's alright
i'm a human being
i'm not god

your touch on my skin

.

luca l. huntzberger

TO APPRECIATE

fries?
no, are you crazy?
pasta?
no, way too much carbs.
dessert?
dude, no.

stop counting on your calories at last.
stop bending to social standards.
stop ruining your life.
that's not healthy.
live in the here and now.
listen to your belly.
think, but don't forbid yourself anything.
you're gonna be all right!
you deserve it.

one year passed and i've learned that appearance is not everything. that loving someone else starts with loving yourself. which is really hard.

that dating should not start with instagram or tinder. that having a personality and deep interest in the other is the real fundament. looking hot is desirable but, in reality, a cool plus.

i really don't care if either my standards are really low, or my priorities are set incorrectly.

all i've learned and now know is that i appreciate me. my body. my personality. my sexuality. and that's the beginning of an open, delightful mindset.

i'm happy with myself. with my decisions. with my change.

it's okay to make mistakes
it's okay not to be sure about your own sexuality
it's okay not to know what to do after school
it's okay to change your opinion
that's called 'being human'
keep that in mind

being selfish seems to be very weird at first sight
feels very unpleasant,
maybe also oppressive
but in fact, when it's about you as a person
about your health
mentally, physically or else
remember that you have the right to be *selfish*.
because you matter.
because you love yourself.
because you appreciate yourself.
because all you want is good.
and everything good starts with you.

your touch on my skin

'am i good enough for this all?
there are people
that would be much better at this
people that are more creative i am
i suck at this
fuck
i shouldn't be doing this art
all i'm doing is tainting it
i'm sorry'

i say when you bring me back to reality
with a slap in the face

i know that you are far away
emotionally and geographically
i know that i think you are very cute
and that i want something from you
and that it's not the other way around
but i'm fine with it

i'm now in a state of mind
where i *accept my feelings*
even though they're challenging
and put a lot of spokes in my wheel

i'm now in a state of mind
where i don't stumble over stones
but kneel down, look at one of them,
appreciate it, take a breath,
stand up and shove it out of my way

sometimes i have weird questions
i wonder what would happen
if i was reborn today
because i love to be that
small little child again
admiring my giant parents
wanting to make them proud
in every way possible
running around the house
on Christmas day
and laughing unconditionally –

i've started this project because of you
i've continued to write about all the things
that came to my mind and
wanted to be written down
because of you

you gave me the strength i needed
you've been my source of motivation
i longed for all the time
yet can't look you in the eyes
because you're still
one of my most beautiful
nightmares

i've longed for that moment
for a very extensive time
to not be dependent anymore
to not be sad anymore
i certainly did it –

i'm lying on my bed
hearing the most beautiful music
i've ever heard
sopranos, harmonies and melodies
the candle's flames playfully dancing
mounting higher and higher into the air
when i have the feeling
i can absorb all of that
and become much stronger
by every second passing

dear diary,
life is very exhausting
every day, we'll encounter absolute contrasts
we experience love
we experience hate
we experience joy
we experience grief
we experience warmth
we experience cold
we experience high
we experience low –
thank you for giving me the chance to
put my worries aside
to process
and to progress
you were a lifelong companion for me
but now it's time to end this first chapter here.
thank you for all
x luca

2019 taught me that
to take full advantage of the
peaceful and beautiful moments
2019 taught me that
no matter when
i'll be able to see the light
at the end of the tunnel
even if sometimes
it seems so impossible
now i can really say
2019 taught me great stuff

luca l. huntzberger

let me tell you:
it's great to go through various phases
where you will never stand still
being constantly refreshed
and experiencing something new
because standing still is always
making a step back

being yourself can be really hard sometimes. it can truly suck because you think you are a piece of shit since you don't behave like your friends do or just because you don't feel right in society

indeed: being different can seem really frightening and terrifying. a fear just like a giant mountain which you have to climb up. because there is no way back or no other possibilities to your desired target.

it's currently raining and storming. you feel the wet on your shoulders which is continuously feeling heavier and heavier. but for a brief moment, you can clearly see the sun on the mountain's other side. you know it'll be better and brighter over there, even though it'll be a hard and rocky road. even though this adventure takes a lot of time - you know that you'll be happy over there.

so, you gather all your courage and make the first step on the steep hill. and the next one. another one. so many steps that you left the rain and the storm behind and now can spot a rainbow some meters in front of you.

a rainbow that encourages and welcomes you to the new world. to a better place. with many differences, many colors, pride, and joy.

getting caught ...

sometimes it's as horrible
as you imagine, yes
especially when you're young and insecure

but it also can be a *sudden relief*
making your life much, much
easier with the next blink

the author

i kept wondering what this could be about. what to say when the writing process is done. the book finally finished.

to this day, i still don't know what to say. this book contains all my energy, all my feelings, all my thoughts towards the people i've met over the last years.
it's one of my biggest secrets that is now going to be accessible for everyone.

what i can say is that i hope you've had a great journey to this page. i really thank you for buying this book and believing in me.

- luca l. huntzberger

luca l. huntzberger is eighteen years old and is currently living in germany, near frankfurt.
ever since he was a little boy, he knew that he liked writing stories. soon, he found out that writing poems was a matter of fate. it just fit.
his goal for the future is to start studying psychology.

find him on social media:

instagram: lucahuntzberger
youtube: luca huntzberger
twitter: lucahuntzberger

no more hostility towards others.
no more hate speech.
no more toxic people.
no more unnecessary sadness.

maybe these resolutions will be fulfilled someday —